How Much Land Does a Man Need?

The Deadly Price of Greed and the Illusion of More

A Modern Translation

Adapted for the Contemporary Reader

Leo Tolstoy

Translated by Tim Zengerink

Table of Contents

Preface - Message to the Reader

What If You Could Help Rebuild the Greatest Library in Human History?

Thousands of years ago, the Library of Alexandria stood as the crown jewel of human achievement — a sanctuary where the collected wisdom of every known civilization was gathered, preserved, and shared freely.

And then, it was lost.

Through fire, conquest, and the slow erosion of time, humanity lost not just books — but ideas, dreams, discoveries, and stories that could have changed the world forever.

Today, the Library of Alexandria lives again — and you are invited to be a part of its restoration.

Our mission is simple yet profound:

To rebuild the greatest library the world has ever known, and to translate all timeless works into every language and dialect, so that no seeker of knowledge is ever left behind again.

By joining our movement to rebuild the modern Library of Alexandria, you become part of an unprecedented mission:

- **Unlimited Access to the Greatest Audiobooks & eBooks Ever Written:**

  Instantly explore thousands of legendary works—Plato, Shakespeare, Jane Austen, Leo Tolstoy, and countless more. All instantly available to read or listen, placing a complete literary universe at your fingertips.

- **Beautiful Paperback & Deluxe Editions at Printing Cost**

  Own any title as an elegant paperback, deluxe hardcover, or stunning collectible boxset—offered to you at true printing cost, delivered straight to your door. Build your personal Library of Alexandria, crafted for beauty, built for durability, and worthy of proud display.

- **Fresh Translations for Modern Readers—in Every Language & Dialect**

  Enjoy timeless masterpieces reimagined in clear, contemporary language—no more outdated phrases or obscure references. Alongside the original versions, we're tirelessly translating these classics into every language and dialect imaginable, ensuring accessibility and understanding across cultures and generations.

- **Join a Global Renaissance of Literature & Knowledge**

  You directly support expanding our library, publishing deluxe editions at true cost, translating works into all global languages, and bringing humanity's greatest stories to people everywhere. By joining today, you're not just preserving a legacy of masterpieces; you set in motion a powerful wave of literary accessibility.

Become a Torchbearer of Knowledge.

Join us for free now at **LibraryofAlexandria.com**

Together, we will ensure that the light of human wisdom never fades again.

With gratitude and a shared love of knowledge,

The Modern Library of Alexandria Team

Visit:

www.libraryofalexandria.com

Or scan the code below:

Introduction

Greed, Simplicity, and
the Fatal Temptation of More

Leo Tolstoy's How Much Land Does a Man Need? is one of the most succinct and powerful parables ever written about the corrosive nature of greed. First published in 1886, this compact narrative continues to resonate across cultures and centuries because it taps into a universal truth: the human tendency to overreach, to grasp beyond necessity, and to confuse abundance with happiness. In less than ten pages, Tolstoy constructs a devastating moral drama that cuts to the heart of modern consumer culture, individual ambition, and the spiritual cost of endless acquisition.

At the center of the story is Pahom, a peasant who is discontented with his modest means and believes that with just a little more land, he could achieve real freedom and peace. As the story unfolds, he is offered increasingly larger tracts of land—first through purchase, then through settlement—and finally, through a seemingly generous offer by a non-Russian tribe, the Bashkirs. They tell him he can have as much land as he can walk around in a single day, provided he returns to the starting point before sunset. Pahom, driven by desire for more, overestimates his strength. By the time he completes the circuit, he collapses and dies from exhaustion. The final line delivers the story's fatal verdict: "Six feet from his head to his heels was all he needed."

This grim punchline transforms what could have been a rural anecdote into a timeless fable. The story is simple but layered, accessible but profound. It is not merely a critique of economic greed—it is a philosophical meditation on mortality, contentment, and the illusion of control. Pahom's tragedy is not that he wanted to improve his life, but that he could not recognize when he had enough. In that sense, he is a reflection of society itself: always striving, always expanding, and always blind to the spiritual emptiness at the core of excessive materialism.

Tolstoy's Moral Vision and the Radical Challenge of Simplicity

Tolstoy wrote How Much Land Does a Man Need? during a period of deep moral and spiritual transformation. In the 1880s, following the publication of his masterpieces War and Peace and Anna Karenina, he experienced an existential crisis. Disillusioned by the excesses of wealth, power, and organized religion, he began to adopt a radical Christian ethic rooted in nonviolence, humility, and ascetic living. He renounced his aristocratic status and sought to live a life of simplicity, labor, and moral clarity. This story, like many others from his later period, reflects that shift.

For Tolstoy, land ownership was not simply a social or economic issue—it was a moral one. In Pahom's obsessive desire to acquire land, we see a microcosm of the Russian aristocracy's domination over the peasantry, the colonial expansion of empires, and the human tendency to treat the Earth as a resource to be conquered rather than a home to be shared. Pahom's downfall illustrates what Tolstoy believed to be a spiritual law: that true freedom is found not in possession, but in relinquishment.

Throughout the story, Tolstoy maintains a deceptively light tone. The prose is clear and direct. The rural setting feels familiar and grounded. The characters are believable, and the narrative unfolds with the inevitability of a folk tale. But beneath this simplicity lies a challenge that remains radical even today. Tolstoy is not merely telling a cautionary tale—he is asking us to reconsider our entire relationship with desire. What if we did not need more to be happy? What if the pursuit of more is precisely what leads to suffering? What if enough is truly enough?

This modern translation preserves the clarity and resonance of Tolstoy's original while updating its language for contemporary readers. It aims to communicate the force of Tolstoy's insight without diluting the gravity of his message. Every sentence is rendered with the goal of awakening the reader's conscience, not merely their appreciation for literary style.

In conclusion, How Much Land Does a Man Need? is more than a short story. It is a spiritual test. It asks each of us to examine the limits of our own desires and to confront the quiet desperation that often drives us to accumulate, expand, and overreach. Pahom's fate is not just a warning for the greedy—it is a mirror for every reader who has ever said, "Just a little more." Tolstoy's answer, delivered with piercing simplicity, is as relevant now as it was in 1886: more is never enough, and in the end, all we need is enough to be buried in. The rest is illusion.

Chapter I

An older sister went to visit her younger sister in the countryside. The older one was married to a businessman in the city, while the younger was married to a farmer in a village. As they sat together drinking tea, the older sister started talking about how great life in the city was. She boasted about their comfortable home, their stylish clothes, the nice outfits her children wore, and all the delicious food they enjoyed. She also talked about going to theaters, parks, and fancy gatherings.

The younger sister felt annoyed and started defending her way of life.

"I wouldn't trade my life for yours," she said. "We may not live in luxury, but at least we don't have constant worries. You might have more than we do, but one bad day could take everything away. You know the saying, 'Wealth and loss go hand in hand.' Many people are rich one day and begging the next. Our life may be simple, but it's stable. We'll never be wealthy, but we'll always have food to eat."

The older sister smirked.

"Food?" she said. "Sure, if you're happy eating with the pigs and cows! What do you know about style or good manners? No matter how hard your husband works, you'll always live in the dirt, and so will your children."

"So what?" the younger sister replied. "Yes, our work is tough, but it's honest. We don't have to answer to anyone. In the city, there are so many dangers—one day, your husband might be doing well, but the next, he could lose everything to gambling, drinking, or other temptations. Doesn't that happen all the time?"

Pahom, the man of the house, was lying on top of the stove, listening to their conversation.

"She's right," he thought. "We peasants work hard from childhood, always busy farming the land, so we don't have time to get caught up in foolishness. Our only problem is that we don't have enough land. If I had plenty of land, I wouldn't have to worry about anything—not even the Devil himself!"

The women finished their tea, talked a little more about clothes, then cleaned up and went to bed.

But the Devil had been sitting behind the stove, listening to everything. He was pleased that the farmer's wife had made her husband so proud that he had dared to say he wouldn't fear even the Devil if he had enough land.

"Very well," thought the Devil. "Let's put that to the test. I'll give you all the land you want—and through it, I will make you mine."

Chapter II

Not far from the village, there was a woman who owned a small piece of land, about three hundred acres. She had always gotten along well with the villagers, but things changed when she hired a new manager—an old soldier—who started giving out heavy fines for the smallest mistakes.

No matter how careful Pahom was, problems kept happening. One day, his horse got into her oat field. Another time, his cow wandered into her garden. Then his calves ended up in her meadow. Each time, he had to pay a fine.

Pahom paid, but it made him angry. He often came home upset and took out his frustration on his family. That summer, the manager caused him so much trouble that he was actually glad when winter came and the animals had to stay inside. Even though feeding them was expensive, at least he didn't have to worry about them getting into trouble anymore.

That winter, word spread that the woman was planning to sell her land, and the innkeeper from the main road was trying to buy it. The villagers became worried.

"If the innkeeper buys the land, things will be even worse than they were with the manager," they thought. "We all depend on that land."

The villagers decided to go together and ask the landowner not to sell the land to the innkeeper. Instead, they offered to buy it themselves at a better price. She agreed.

At first, they tried to buy the land as a group, so everyone could share it. But after two meetings, they couldn't come to an agreement. They argued over how to divide it, and no one could agree on what was fair. So they decided that each family would buy as much land as they could afford. The landowner was fine with this plan too.

Not long after, Pahom heard that one of his neighbors had bought fifty acres. The landowner had agreed to take half the payment right away and the rest within a year. Pahom felt jealous.

"Look at that," he thought. "The land is getting sold, and I'll be left with nothing."

He turned to his wife.

"Everyone else is buying land, so we should too," he said. "Living here is getting too hard. That manager is making things worse with all these fines."

Together, they figured out how to gather enough money. They had saved a hundred roubles. To raise more, they sold a young horse and half of their beehives, sent one of their sons to work for wages in advance, and borrowed the rest from a relative. In the end, they scraped together half the amount needed.

Pahom picked out a forty-acre farm, which included some forested land, and went to the landowner to negotiate. They agreed on a price, shook hands, and he paid a deposit. They traveled to town to sign the paperwork, with Pahom paying half upfront and promising to pay the rest within two years.

Now, Pahom had land of his own. He borrowed seeds and planted crops. That year, the harvest was good, and within a year, he had paid off all his debts to both the landowner and his brother-in-law.

He was now a landowner. He plowed and planted his own fields, made hay from his own land, cut trees from his own forest, and fed his animals in his own pastures. Every time he went out to work on his land or look at his growing crops, he felt overjoyed. The grass, the flowers, and the fields all seemed more beautiful than before. He had walked past that land many times in the past without giving it much thought, but now, it felt special.

Chapter III

Pahom was happy with his land, but there was one problem—his neighbors kept letting their animals wander onto his fields and pastures. He asked them politely to stop, but they didn't listen. The village herdsmen allowed cows to graze on his land, and horses from the night pasture trampled his crops. Pahom chased them away over and over, forgiving their owners each time. For a while, he avoided taking legal action, but eventually, he lost patience and took the matter to court.

Pahom knew his neighbors weren't trying to harm him on purpose—they just didn't have enough land of their own. But he thought, "If I don't do something, they'll ruin everything I have. They need to learn a lesson."

So he filed complaints, and a few villagers were fined. After that, the others started to resent him. Some even began letting their cattle onto his land on purpose. One night, someone snuck into his woods and cut down five young lime trees for their bark.

One day, as Pahom walked through his woods, he noticed something pale on the ground. As he got closer, he saw tree stumps and the trunks lying nearby, stripped of their bark. He was furious.

"If they had taken just one, it would still be bad," he thought. "But they cut down a whole patch! If I find out who did this, I'll make sure they regret it."

He tried to figure out who was responsible. After thinking it over, he decided it must have been Simon. He went to Simon's house to search for proof, but he found nothing, and their argument ended in anger. Still, Pahom was convinced Simon was guilty, so he took him to court.

The case was heard multiple times, but in the end, Simon was found innocent due to lack of evidence. Pahom was furious and accused the village elder and judges of corruption.

"You're all taking bribes!" he shouted. "If you were honest, you wouldn't let thieves walk free."

Because of this, Pahom quarreled with both the judges and his neighbors. Rumors spread that someone might set fire to his home. Although he now had more land, he was no longer welcome in the village like before.

Around this time, he heard people talking about new settlements.

"I don't need to move," Pahom thought. "But if some families leave, there will be more land for me. I could buy their fields and make my farm bigger. That would make life much easier. Right now, I still don't have enough space."

One evening, a traveling peasant stopped by Pahom's house, looking for a place to stay the night. Pahom welcomed him, shared a meal, and asked where he was from.

The man explained that he had been working beyond the Volga River, where many people were settling. He told Pahom that peasants from his village had moved there and joined a new community. Each family was given twenty-five acres of land for free, and anyone with money could buy even more. He described how the soil was so fertile that rye grew as tall as a horse and thick enough that five swings of a sickle would cut a full bundle. One poor man arrived with nothing but his hands and now owned six horses and two cows.

Hearing this, Pahom's heart burned with excitement.

"Why should I stay here and struggle when life is so much better elsewhere?" he thought. "I'll sell my land and house, take the money, and start fresh over there.

In this village, there are always problems. But first, I need to see it for myself."

By summer, Pahom was ready to go. He traveled down the Volga River by steamboat to Samara, then walked another three hundred miles on foot before reaching the settlement.

Everything was just as the traveler had described. The villagers had plenty of land, each person receiving twenty-five acres of communal land to use. Those who had money could buy as much private land as they wanted for only fifty cents an acre.

Satisfied with what he had learned, Pahom returned home in the fall and started selling his belongings. He sold his land for a profit, gave up his house and livestock, and withdrew from the village community. He waited until spring, then packed up his family and set off for his new home.

Chapter IV

When Pahom and his family reached their new home, he applied to join the local village community. To gain approval, he hosted a feast for the village elders and completed the necessary paperwork. He was given five shares of communal land for himself and his sons, totaling 125 acres, though the plots were scattered in different locations. He also had the right to use the communal pasture for his livestock.

Pahom built the farm structures he needed and bought livestock. He now had three times more land than before, and the soil was rich and fertile. His situation was much better than in his old village. He had plenty of farmland and pasture, and he could keep as many animals as he wanted.

At first, Pahom was happy as he settled into his new life, but after a while, he started feeling like even this land wasn't enough.

The first year, he planted wheat on his share of the communal land and had a great harvest. He wanted to keep planting wheat, but he didn't have enough land for it. In that area, wheat could only be grown on fresh or unused land. After one or two years, the fields needed to rest until prairie grass grew back. Many villagers wanted this type of land, and there wasn't enough for everyone. This led to arguments—wealthier peasants wanted the land to plant wheat, while poorer ones preferred to rent it out to traders to earn money for taxes.

Since Pahom wanted to plant more wheat, he rented land from a trader for a year. He had a good harvest, but the field was more than ten miles from his home, which made transportation difficult.

After some time, he noticed that certain peasant traders were living on their own farms instead of in the village, and they were becoming wealthy. He thought, "If I could buy my own land and build a home on it, everything would be in one place, and life would be much easier."

The idea of owning his own land kept coming back to him.

For three years, he continued renting land and planting wheat. The seasons were good, and his harvests were plentiful, so he started saving money. He could have been content, but he grew tired of constantly having to rent land and compete for the best fields. Whenever a good piece of land became available, villagers rushed to claim it, and unless you acted fast, you got nothing.

In his third year, he and a trader rented a piece of pasture from some peasants. They had already plowed it when a dispute broke out, and the peasants took the matter to court. In the end, the deal fell apart, and all their hard work was wasted.

"If I had my own land," Pahom thought, "I wouldn't have to deal with all this trouble. I could be independent."

So he started searching for land to buy. Eventually, he found a peasant who owned 1,300 acres but was struggling financially and willing to sell at a low price. Pahom negotiated and bargained until they agreed on a price—1,500 roubles, with part of the payment upfront and the rest later.

Just as Pahom was about to close the deal, a traveling trader stopped by his house to rest his horse. They sat down for tea, and during their conversation, the trader mentioned that he had just returned from the land of the Bashkirs, far away. There, he had bought 13,000 acres for only 1,000 roubles—much cheaper than the land Pahom was about to buy.

Pahom was curious and asked more questions.

The trader explained, "All you need to do is make friends with the Bashkir chiefs. I gave them about 100 roubles' worth of gifts—some fine robes, carpets, a box of tea, and wine for those who wanted it. In exchange, I got the land for less than two cents an acre."

He pulled out the official documents to prove his claim and added, "The land is near a river, and the entire prairie is untouched, with rich, fertile soil."

Pahom kept asking questions, and the trader went on, "There is more land there than you could ever walk across in a year. The Bashkirs own all of it, and they are simple people. You can get land from them for almost nothing."

Pahom's mind started racing.

"Why should I pay 1,500 roubles for just 1,300 acres and still be in debt? If I go there, I can get more than ten times as much land for the same price!"

Chapter V

Pahom asked for directions to the place, and as soon as the trader left, he got ready for the journey. He left his wife in charge of their home and set off, bringing along one of his workers. On the way, they stopped in a town to buy a case of tea, some wine, and other gifts, just as the trader had suggested.

They traveled over 300 miles, and on the seventh day, they reached the land where the Bashkirs had set up their tents. Everything was exactly as the trader had described. The Bashkirs lived on the open plains near a river in tents covered with felt. They didn't farm or eat bread. Instead, their cattle and horses roamed freely, grazing on the grasslands. Young horses were tied behind the tents, and the mares were brought to them twice a day to be milked. The women made a drink called kumiss from the milk and also prepared cheese.

The men, on the other hand, spent their days drinking kumiss and tea, eating mutton, and playing music. They were cheerful and carefree, never worrying about work during the summer. They didn't know Russian and had little knowledge of the outside world, but they were friendly and welcoming.

As soon as they spotted Pahom, they came out of their tents and gathered around him. Someone who spoke both languages was found to translate, and Pahom explained that he had come to buy land.

The Bashkirs were excited to hear this. They led Pahom to one of their best tents, where they seated him on soft cushions placed over a carpet. They served him tea and kumiss and even slaughtered a sheep to prepare a meal of fresh mutton.

Pahom then took out the gifts he had brought and shared them among the Bashkirs, giving them the tea as well. The Bashkirs were overjoyed. They chatted excitedly among themselves before turning to the interpreter to pass on a message.

"They want you to know," the interpreter said, "that they like you and that it is our custom to make guests happy and repay them for their kindness. You have given us gifts, so now tell us what you like best among the things we have, and we will gladly give it to you."

Pahom thought for a moment, then replied, "What I like most here is your land. Back home, the land is crowded, and the soil is no longer good. But here, you have plenty of land, and it's the best I've ever seen."

The interpreter translated his words, and the Bashkirs began talking excitedly again. Pahom couldn't understand what they were saying, but he could tell they found something amusing because they laughed and shouted among themselves. Then, after a moment, they quieted down and turned to listen as the interpreter spoke again.

"They say that since you have given them gifts, they are happy to give you as much land as you want. You only need to point it out, and it will be yours."

The Bashkirs then started talking among themselves again, this time with more serious expressions.

Pahom asked what they were discussing, and the interpreter explained, "Some believe we should wait for our chief to return before making a decision. Others think there's no need to wait and that we can go ahead without him."

Chapter VI

As the Bashkirs were arguing, a man wearing a large fur hat appeared. Everyone instantly stopped talking and stood up. The interpreter turned to Pahom and said, "This is our leader."

Pahom quickly brought out his finest robe and five pounds of tea, offering them as a gift. The Chief accepted the presents and sat down in the place of honor. The Bashkirs eagerly began speaking to him. He listened for a while, then raised his head, signaling them to be quiet. Then, speaking in Russian, he said to Pahom,

"Alright. Pick any piece of land you want—we have plenty," the Chief said.

Pahom felt excited but also a little worried. "I can't just take land without proof," he thought. "What if they say it's mine today but change their minds later? I need to make sure it's officially mine."

Out loud, he said, "Thank you for your generosity. You have so much land, and I only need a little. But I want to be sure which part belongs to me. Could it be measured and legally given to me? Life is unpredictable—while you offer it freely now, your children might want it back someday."

The Chief nodded. "You're right. We will make it official."

Pahom continued, "I heard that a trader came before me, and you gave him land with proper documents. I would like to do the same."

The Chief understood.

"Yes," he said. "That's easy. We have a scribe who can write the agreement, and we will go to town with you to get it properly sealed."

"How much will it cost?" Pahom asked.

"Our price is always the same—one thousand roubles per day."

Pahom was confused.

"A day? What do you mean? How much land is that?"

The Chief shrugged. "We don't measure in acres. We sell land by the day. However much land you can walk around in one day is yours—for one thousand roubles."

Pahom was shocked.

"But in a full day, a person could walk around a huge amount of land!" he said.

The Chief laughed. "Then all of it will be yours! But there is one rule—if you don't return to the starting point by sunset, you lose your money and get nothing."

"How will I mark the land I walk around?" Pahom asked.

"It's simple," the Chief explained. "We will go to the starting point and wait for you there. You will carry a spade. As you walk, dig small holes and place pieces of turf in them to mark the land. At every turn, dig another hole. Later, we will use a plow to connect the marks. You can walk as far as you like, but you must return to the starting point before the sun sets. Whatever land you cover will be yours."

Pahom was thrilled. They agreed to begin at sunrise the next day.

After talking for a while longer, they had more kumiss, ate more mutton, and drank tea again. As night fell, the Bashkirs gave Pahom a soft feather bed to sleep on. Then they all went to rest, promising to gather at daybreak and ride out to the chosen spot before sunrise.

Chapter VII

Pahom lay on the soft feather bed, but he couldn't sleep. His mind kept spinning with thoughts about the land.

"I'm going to claim a huge area!" he thought. "I can easily walk thirty-five miles in a day. The days are long now, and that will give me plenty of land! I can sell the rough parts or rent them to peasants, but I'll keep the best land for myself and farm it. I'll buy two teams of oxen and hire two workers. I'll plant crops on about 150 acres and use the rest for grazing cattle."

He stayed awake all night, finally dozing off just before dawn. But as soon as he fell asleep, he had a strange and disturbing dream.

In the dream, he was lying in the same tent when he heard someone laughing outside. Curious, he got up to see who it was. Stepping outside, he saw the Bashkir Chief sitting in front of the tent, laughing so hard he was holding his sides.

Pahom was confused. "What's so funny?" he asked. But as he looked closer, he realized it wasn't the Chief— it was the trader who had come to his house and told him about the land. Just as Pahom was about to ask,

"How long have you been here?" the trader suddenly changed.

Now, he looked like the peasant who had once traveled from the Volga to Pahom's old village. But in the next moment, the peasant changed again.

Pahom gasped as he saw the Devil himself sitting there, chuckling, with horns and hooves. In front of him, lying barefoot on the ground, was a man dressed only in a simple shirt and trousers.

Pahom squinted, trying to see who it was. His heart froze. The man on the ground was himself—dead.

He woke up in shock, his heart racing.

"What a strange dream," he thought, trying to push away his fear.

He turned and saw the first light of dawn coming through the tent door.

"It's time to wake everyone up," he told himself. "We need to get going."

He got up and shook his servant awake.

"Get the horses ready," he said.

Then he went to call the Bashkirs.

"It's time to go measure the land," he told them.

The Bashkirs got up and gathered together. Their Chief arrived as well. But before leaving, they started drinking kumiss again and offered Pahom some tea.

"Let's go already!" he said impatiently. "We're wasting time!"

Chapter VIII

The Bashkirs got ready, and they all set off—some riding horses, others traveling in carts. Pahom rode in his small cart with his servant, carrying a spade. As they reached the open plains, the sky glowed with the soft light of morning.

They climbed a small hill, which the Bashkirs called a shikhan, and came to a stop. Everyone got down from their carts and horses, gathering in one spot. The Chief stretched out his arm, pointing toward the vast land in front of them.

"Look," he said, "all of this, as far as you can see, belongs to us. You can choose any part of it for yourself."

Pahom's eyes lit up with excitement. The land was untouched, smooth, and full of rich, dark soil. In the lower areas, tall grasses grew thick and wild.

The Chief took off his fur hat, placed it on the ground, and said, "This will be the starting point. Begin here and return to this exact spot. All the land you walk around will be yours."

Pahom took out his money and set it on the Chief's hat. Then he removed his outer coat, keeping only his sleeveless undershirt. He tightened his belt, put a small bag of bread inside his coat, and tied a flask of water to his waist. Pulling up his boots, he took the spade from his servant and got ready.

He paused for a moment, thinking about which direction to take. "The land is good in every direction, so it doesn't really matter," he decided. "I'll walk toward the rising sun."

He stretched, faced east, and waited for the sun to rise above the horizon.

"I can't waste time," he thought. "It's best to walk while the air is still cool."

As soon as the first rays of sunlight appeared, Pahom threw the spade over his shoulder and stepped onto the open plains.

He walked at a steady pace, not too fast or too slow. After about a thousand yards, he stopped, dug a hole, and placed pieces of grass inside to mark the spot. Then he kept going. As his body warmed up, he picked up speed and, after some time, dug another hole.

Looking back, he could still see the small hill, the people standing on it, and the sunlight reflecting off the metal rims of the carts.

"I must have walked about three miles," he thought.

The day was getting hotter. He took off his undershirt, threw it over his shoulder, and kept moving. After a while, he glanced at the sun's position and thought,

"I should eat something. The first stretch is done, but I still have three more to go. It's too soon to turn back. I'll just take off my boots to make walking easier."

He sat down, pulled off his boots, tucked them into his belt, and continued walking. The ground felt softer beneath his feet, making each step lighter.

"I'll walk another three miles before turning left," Pahom thought. "This land is so good—it would be a waste not to take as much as I can. The further I go, the better it looks."

He kept moving forward, but when he glanced back, the small hill was barely visible. The people on it looked like tiny black dots, and the only thing that stood out was a faint glimmer of sunlight reflecting off the carts.

"I've gone far enough in this direction," he told himself. "It's time to turn. I'm sweating and really thirsty."

He stopped, dug a deep hole, and stacked up pieces of grass to mark the spot. Then he untied his flask, took a drink, and turned left.

The tall grass brushed against him as he walked, and the heat became unbearable. Pahom started to feel exhausted. He looked at the sun—it was already noon.

"I need a break," he thought.

He sat down, ate some bread, and drank more water. But he didn't lie down, afraid that if he did, he might fall asleep. After a short rest, he forced himself to get back up and keep going.

At first, he felt fine. The food gave him energy. But as the heat rose, he started feeling sluggish and sleepy.

"Just one more hour of discomfort," he told himself, "and I'll have land for the rest of my life."

He continued walking in the same direction for a long time before getting ready to turn left again. But just as he was about to, he noticed a low, damp area in the distance.

"That would be a great place to grow flax," he thought. "I can't leave it out."

So he kept going past the hollow, marked another spot on the other side, and then finally made his turn.

Looking back at the hill, he saw the air shimmering from the heat, making it hard to see clearly. The people waiting there were nothing more than faint, blurry shapes.

"I've made my route too long," he realized. "I need to shorten this last stretch."

He started walking along the third side of the square, moving faster now. He glanced at the sun and saw it had already dropped lower in the sky. He had covered almost two miles on the third stretch, but there were still about ten miles left before he reached the starting point.

"I can't keep walking in a square," he thought. "If I try to make the shape perfect, I might go too far and run out of time. I already have plenty of land—I need to go straight back now."

Quickly, he dug another hole, marked it, and turned straight toward the small hill, rushing back as fast as he could.

Chapter IX

Pahom headed straight for the hill, but every step became harder. The heat had drained his energy, his bare feet were bruised and cut, and his legs felt weak. He wanted to stop and rest, but he couldn't—if he didn't make it back before sunset, all his effort would be wasted. The sun kept sinking lower and lower.

"Oh no," he thought, "did I make a huge mistake trying to take too much? What if I don't make it in time?"

He looked at the hill in the distance, then at the sun. He was still far from the finish line, and the sun was nearly touching the horizon. He pushed forward, but his body was exhausted. Desperate, he started running. He threw off his coat, kicked away his boots, dropped his flask and cap—keeping only his spade to lean on.

"What have I done?" he thought. "I was too greedy, and now I might lose everything. I'll never get there in time!"

The fear made his breath come in short gasps. His wet clothes clung to him, his mouth was dry, and his chest heaved like a bellows. His heart pounded like a hammer, and his legs barely held him up. Panic set in—what if he died from the effort?

Even though his body was giving up, he couldn't stop. "After running all this way, I can't quit now. Everyone would think I'm a fool," he told himself.

The voices of the Bashkirs echoed across the plain. They were shouting and waving at him to hurry. Their cries pushed him forward. He gathered every bit of strength he had left and ran as fast as he could.

The sun was huge and red, touching the edge of the sky. It was about to disappear! He was so close—he could see the people on the hill waving their arms. He saw the Chief sitting near the fur hat where his money lay. Suddenly, his dream flashed in his mind.

"There's so much land," he thought, "but what's the point if I don't survive? I've ruined everything... I'm not going to make it!"

He looked at the sun. Half of it had already disappeared behind the horizon. With his last ounce of strength, he lunged forward, his legs barely keeping up with his body. Just as he reached the hill, darkness fell.

He lifted his head and saw—the sun was gone.

A sharp cry escaped his lips. "All my effort was for nothing," he thought. He was about to stop, but then he heard the Bashkirs still cheering. He realized that from where they stood on the hill, they could still see the sun.

Taking one last breath, he forced himself up the hill. The moment he reached the top, he saw the cap and the Chief laughing. His dream flashed before him again, and a wave of terror filled him.

With a final gasp, his legs gave out. He collapsed, his hands touching the cap.

"What a powerful man!" the Chief said. "He has claimed so much land!"

Pahom's servant rushed to him and tried to lift him, but it was too late. Blood dripped from Pahom's mouth—he was dead.

The Bashkirs shook their heads and sighed in pity.

His servant picked up the spade and dug a grave just big enough for Pahom to fit in. In the end, all the land he truly needed was six feet from head to toe.

Thank You for Reading

Dear Reader,

We hope this timeless classic has sparked your imagination and enriched your literary journey. Now that you've turned the final page, we want to share a vision for the future of reading—one where every classic you've ever wanted to explore is at your fingertips, in a format that best suits your life.

We'd like to invite you to gain immediate, unlimited digital & audiobook access to hundreds of the most treasured literary classics ever written—along with the option to secure deluxe paperback, hardcover & box set editions at printing cost. Together, we can spark a new global literary renaissance alongside our small, independent publishing house called "The Library of Alexandria."

Thousands of years ago, the Library of Alexandria stood as a beacon of knowledge—until it was lost to history. We aim to reignite that spirit of preservation and discovery right now, in the modern age—only this time, it's accessible to all, in every language and every format.

Picture a world where every timeless classic, novel, poem, or philosophical treatise is not only available to read but also updated for today's readers—modernized, translated into any language or dialect, and ready to enjoy in any format you choose, whether that is in an eBook, audiobook, paperback, or deluxe hardcover & box set version a printing cost.

By joining our movement to rebuild the modern Library of Alexandria, you become part of an unprecedented mission to offer:

- **Unlimited Audiobook & eBook Access to the Greatest Classics of All Time**

  Instantly explore thousands of legendary works, from Plato and Shakespeare to Jane Austen and Leo Tolstoy. All are instantly ready to read or listen to, giving you a complete literary universe at your fingertips.

- **Paperback & Deluxe Editions at Printing Costs:**

  Purchase any title in a paperback, deluxe hardbound, or deluxe boxset edition at printing costs, shipped right to your doorstep. Curate your personal library of Alexandria with editions worthy of display— crafted to last, designed to captivate, and delivered straight to your door.

- **Modern translations for Contemporary Readers in all languages and dialects**

  Discover a vast selection of classics reimagined in clear, current language—no more struggling with outdated phrases or obscure references. Next to the original versions, we aim to offer translations in as many languages and dialects as possible.

  As we continue our translation efforts and add new languages, readers everywhere can connect with these works as if they were written today. By bridging linguistic divides, you're contributing to ensuring that these timeless stories become more meaningful, accessible, and inspiring for people across the globe.

- **Your Personal Library of Alexandria:**

  Over the months and years, you'll curate a unique physical archive of classics—each volume a testament to your taste, curiosity, and love of knowledge. It's not just about owning books—it's about curating a cultural legacy you'll cherish and pass down for generations to come.

- **Join a Global Literary Renaissance:**

  Your support fuels an ongoing mission: allowing us to reinvest in offering deluxe print editions (including special boxsets) at their true cost, broaden the range of available formats and translations, and extend the reach of these works to new audiences worldwide. By joining today, you're not just preserving a legacy of masterpieces; you set in motion a powerful wave of literary accessibility.

We are more than a publisher—we're a movement, and we can't do it alone. Your support lets us scale our mission, preserving and reimagining history's greatest works for tomorrow's readers.

Become a Torchbearer of knowledge.

Thank you for picking up this book and allowing us into your literary journey. As you turn the pages, know that you're part of something larger: a global effort to keep these stories alive, share their wisdom across borders and generations, and spark a true cultural revival for the modern era.

If this resonates with you—please consider taking the next step by visiting:

www.libraryofalexandria.com

With gratitude and a shared love of knowledge,

The Modern Library of Alexandria Team

Visit:

www.libraryofalexandria.com

Or scan the code below: